Puss 'n Boots

Retold by Trina Lawrence
Illustrated by Michelle Morse

Pioneer Valley Educational Press, Inc.

There once was an old miller
who died and left all his property
to his three sons. He left a mill
to his eldest son, a donkey
to the middle son, and the youngest son
got nothing but a cat.

"What will I do with a cat?"
said the youngest son unhappily.
"I guess I will die of hunger."

"Do not be worried, master," said the cat
who was listening. "If you give me a pair
of boots and a bag, I will make us
a fortune fit for a king."

The young man gave the cat
a bag and his best pair of boots.

The cat immediately used the bag
to trap a rabbit.

He took the rabbit to the king
and said, "Sir, I have brought you
a tasty rabbit from my noble lord,
the Master of Carabas."

"Tell your master," said the king,
"that I thank him, and that
I am very pleased with his gift."

Next, the cat used the bag to trap
some partridges. He took
the partridges to the king
and said, "Sir, I have brought you
some partridges from my noble lord,
the Master of Carabas."

One afternoon, the king was taking a drive along the riverside with his daughter, the most beautiful princess in the world.

The cat said to his master, "If you will follow my advice, your fortune will be made. Go and swim in the river and leave the rest to me."

The young man jumped into the river for a swim. While he was swimming, the cat hid his master's clothes.

Soon, the king and his daughter
passed by the river. The cat began
to cry out, "Help! Help! My lord,
the Master of Carabas
has been robbed!"

"Robbers came and stole
my master's clothes," the cat told the king.

The king sent someone back
to the castle for some clothes.

Soon, the cat's young master
was dressed in some of the
king's finest clothing.

The princess thought
the young man was very handsome.
"Join us on our drive!"
she said to the young man.

As the coach drove along,
the cat ran ahead. He came across
some men working in a field.

"My good fellows, you must tell
the king that the field you are plowing
belongs to my lord, Master of Carabas.
If you do not, you will be chopped up
like mincemeat."

When the coach approached
the field, the king asked,
"Who does this field belong to?"

The men all answered, "It belongs
to our lord, Master of Carabas,"
for the cat's threat had frightened them.

The king was told the same
thing at each field he passed.

At last, the cat came to a big castle
that belonged to an ogre.
The cat knocked on the castle door.

When the ogre answered the door
the cat said, "I have heard that you are
able to change yourself into any kind
of creature. Is it true that you
can change yourself into a lion
or an elephant?"

"It *is* true," replied the ogre.
"And to convince you, I shall now
become a lion." And the ogre
turned into a lion.

The cat, being quite brave, did not flinch.
"Oh, how amazing!" he said.

"Is it true," said the cat,
"that you can also turn yourself
   into the smallest of animals,
   for example, a rat or a mouse?
   I must tell you that I think
   that would be *quite* impossible!"

"Impossible?" cried the ogre.
"You shall see!" He immediately
   changed himself into a mouse
   and began to run about the floor.

As soon as the cat saw this,
   he ran after the mouse
   and ate him up.

When the king's carriage arrived
at the castle, the cat greeted them
at the door. "Welcome to the home
of my noble lord,
the Master of Carabas!" he said.

The king was very impressed
with the castle and all the fields.
The princess married
the cat's young master and
they lived happily ever after
in the ogre's castle. The cat
never again chased after mice
or rats, but instead
spent his days napping in the sun.